W9-CDU-386

Grandmother's Pigeon

Louise Erdrich · Illustrated by Jim LaMarche

Hyperion Books for Children
New York

F I R S T   E D I T I O N
1 3 5 7 9 10 8 6 4 2

The artwork for each picture is prepared
using acrylic and colored pencil on Windsor Newton Paper.
This book is set in 16-point Bernhard Modern.

Library of Congress Cataloging-in-Publication Data

Erdrich, Louise.
Grandmother's pigeon / Louise Erdrich; illustrated by Jim
LaMarche —1st ed.
p.   cm.
Summary: Passenger pigeon hatchlings, thought to be extinct, are
discovered in Grandmother's room after she departs on a voyage to
Greenland.
ISBN 0-7868-0165-4 (trade) — ISBN 0-7868-2137-X (lib. bdg.)
[1. Passenger pigeons—Fiction. 2. Pigeons—Fiction. 3. Extinct
animals—Fiction. 4. Grandmothers—Fiction.] I. LaMarche, Jim,
ill. II. Title
PZ7.E72554Gr   1996
[Fic]—dc20   95-2994

To Pallas—

Gallant, funny, kind
and always living the mystery
—Love Mom

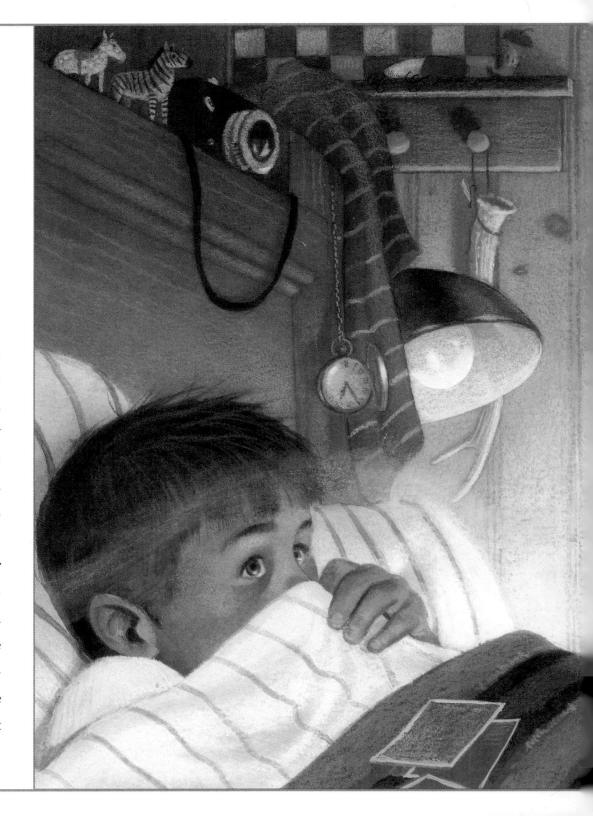

s it turned out, Grandmother was a far more mysterious woman than any of us knew. It was common knowledge that she had trained kicking mules. We'd often heard how she had skied the Continental Divide. I was with her myself once when she turned back a vicious dog by planting herself firm in its path and staring into its eyes.

There was a softer side of Grandmother as well. In her hands there was soothing medicine. She could numb a bruise, touch away a charley horse. When on school test days we felt slightly ill, she brewed a magic tea so bitter that we usually got well just as she brought it into our rooms. Yes, we all thought we knew Grandmother.

Then on our annual beach vacation, as the rest of us basked in the sun, she sailed away on the back of a congenial porpoise.

"Good-bye!" she called. "I've always wanted to see Greenland!"

"But you're heading due west!" my brother shouted, "and besides, this is the Pacific Ocean!"

Grandmother had always been bad on geography, but with a skillful motion of her feet she steered the porpoise south.

"I'll go the scenic route!" she called as she passed out of view, behind a wave. "Round the horn!"

Those were the last words we heard from Grandmother.

One year later, we had to admit, very sadly, that our grandmother had left us for good. Our house was small. My brother wanted to keep her cluttered room as it was, as a shrine, he said. I was undecided, and so was Father. He tousled the hair on his head. In this situation Mother was the firm one, the sensible voice.

"Every time I pass Grandmother's room," she said, "I hear noises. I'm afraid that mice are getting into her possessions. We should at least check and then, maybe, store a few things away in boxes."

She was right, of course, and so with heavy hearts we opened the door to Grandmother's room.

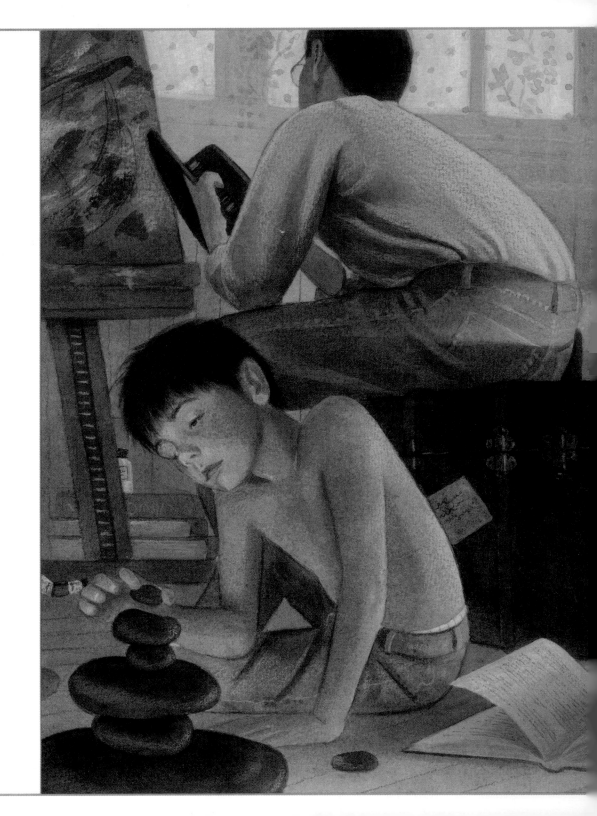

All was as she had left it. There, on the windowsill, behind a curtain of Irish lace, the wooden effigy of Sun-tzu's horse. The smooth black stones that she had collected on the shores of Lake Superior were still neatly stacked in the corner. Over the mantel of the fireplace, where she kept her petrified buffalo tooth, there still hung an original painting by Paul Klee. She had met him on a different beach vacation long ago. The memory of her description of that event brought tears to our eyes, as did the title of one of her many favorite books scattered on the floor, *Consider the Porpoise*.

"Ah," said Father, standing pensively before a shelf, "what a wonderful collection of birds' nests Grandmother has."

We all knew he was trying to divert our attention, and we were grateful. We gathered around him.

The nest made of horsehair was my brother's favorite. I liked the hummingbird's, no bigger than my little fingernail, created with stolen spiderwebs. There was a nest of sticks and yarn, a swallow's nest, the sacklike nest of a Baltimore oriole, a goldfinch nest cunningly woven of milkweed floss and strips of birch bark, and one of rough twigs that contained three eggs.

"How peculiar," said Mother, taking the nest into her hands and nearly dropping it in astonishment when one of the eggs began to hatch.

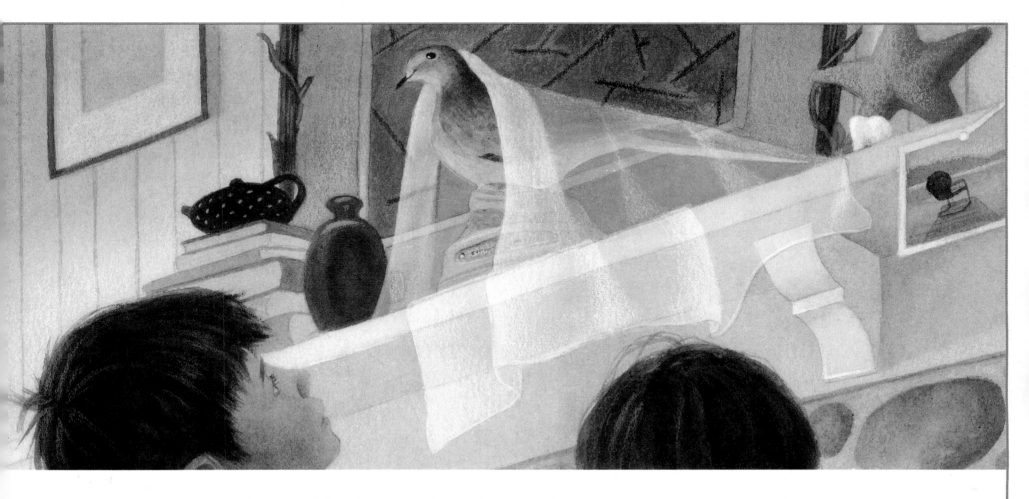

Cradled in the warmth of my mother's fingers, the other eggs began to tremble. Soon tiny beaks had pecked through and, to our fascinated surprise, three hatchlings lay before us.

"An open window!" Father said, a little wildly. "A bird must have flown in!" But upon checking, he found every sash shut tight.

"I can't explain this," Mother muttered over and over, holding the nest and warming the hatchlings with her cupped fingers.

My brother and I stared at each other. Without a word, we turned and sneaked a look at Grandmother's stuffed pigeon. Motionless on its plaster roost, it stared down at us with bright glass eyes. It usually wore a sad expression, but that day it looked very pleased with itself.

Sometimes, at night, I thought I heard it softly cooing. But that may have been the pigeon squabs, too. They grew quickly in Mother's care. She read all that she could find about pigeons. From an eyedropper, she fed them a food that resembled pigeon's milk.

Something about them clearly bothered her, however, and one day she announced to all of us, "I can't stand it anymore. I'm calling an ornithologist."

She did, and one arrived, looking oddly like the birds she studied. Her hair was stuck up in a short gray tuft. She cocked her head one way, then the other, examining our young pigeons. Her eyeglasses made her eyes both round and shrewd. At last she straightened up, regarding all of us.

"Impossible," she stated. "Completely impossible. Yet true."

"What?" my brother demanded. "What's impossible? What's true?"

"It is impossible," said the ornithologist, adjusting her glasses, "that in your kitchen you have raised three members of an extinct species. *Ectopistes migratorius*. These are passenger pigeons. Once upon a time, these birds were so abundant that they traveled in flocks that took three days to pass overhead, 300 million birds per hour. Their nesting colonies sometimes stretched forty miles long. They seemed limitless as leaves."

Her face took on the same grim and sadly surprised look that Grandmother's pigeon usually wore.

"The lesson they teach is this—nature is both tough and fragile. Greed destroyed them. They were killed for food by the millions, and their nesting trees were burned. The last known pigeon, whose name was Martha, died in 1914 in the Cincinnati Zoo. That is, the last pigeon that we knew about! When reality at last sinks in, I shall be in shock. I shall have to sit down. Perhaps I shall sit down now, before I fall over. Have you got any tea?"

In his eagerness to help, our father brewed a cup of Grandmother's bitter medicine. There was no mistaking the odor of singed moth wings. But the taste didn't seem to faze the ornithologist. She drank cup after cup, and we looked at her with new respect.

"With your permission," she stated, "I will call in the head of the Cornell Bird Laboratory. I will do my best to fend off the newspaper and magazine reporters, but once this news breaks it will be difficult."

"Say no more," said Father. "We will find a way to retain our privacy, but the interest of science must be served. You have our permission to call in the experts."

What happened during the next week was exciting but exhausting. Mother tired of explaining over and over how the eggs had hatched as she held the nest. Father became anxious and harassed. There were strangers in the house at all times, and my brother and I often retreated to the tree house that Grandmother had built for us, where we could not be reached by curious interviewers.

One evening, when the last scientist and reporter had finally left, we ran back to the house, hungry for the peace and comfort of our evening dinner. But it was not to be. Mother and Father were sitting at the kitchen table, the pigeon cage before them, and they were having an argument.

"They are all males," said Mother. "The ornithologist said so. She told me, confidentially, that there is no hope of reestablishing the species. None whatsoever. What happened in this house is a fluke, a miracle."

"And yet," said Father, "shouldn't they be studied?"

"But then they would be caged for life!" said Mother. "It seems unfair."

"I see your point," said Father. "I, too, have grown attached to the birds."

We all regarded the pigeons in the cage. The three looked back at us. Their expressions were dull and weary, they didn't hop about or ruffle their feathers. They didn't gurgle, hadn't the strength to coo. Their listless eyes changed Father's mind completely. "They look tired. If they are not set free soon," he said, "well, I worry!"

"Say no more," my brother answered, looking hard at me, and I knew that night we'd put into action the deed we had planned.

White moonlight fell in bands through the kitchen windows and led the way out. We carried the cage between us, set it down in cool wet grass. I held each pigeon as my brother taped onto their spindly pink legs the rolled messages we had penned. And then, as he stroked their tiny heads and whispered soft directions, I lifted my arms and opened my hands.

The escape of the pigeons infuriated many. Our birds were reported heading north, and then all trace of them was lost. There was talk of prosecution. Father stood firm and said we had nothing to apologize for. Even the ornithologist, who had become our friend, declared that the right thing had been done. Mother smiled at my brother and me, and she brushed our hair with fingers touching lightly.

Several weeks passed, and then one day a lime-green envelope fell through the mail slot beside our front door. When Father recognized the writing, he opened the letter with quick and eager fingers. Hastily, he unfolded a piece of pale green paper.

Thank you for your pigeon messages, my dears.
Actually, I've just arrived.
It took much longer than I had planned.
I had to change porpoises three times
and catch a whale.
I do apologize for not writing enroute,
but I simply found myself too busy.
Greenland is interesting,
the people friendly, but I miss all of you,
and home.
I'll come back soon!
Love, Grandmother
P.S. Be careful with my stuffed pigeon . . .